THE FACE
AT THE WINDOW

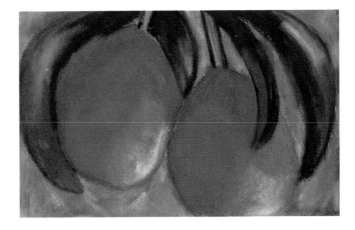

by REGINA HANSON
Illustrated by LINDA SAPORT

Clarion Books ◆ *New York*

The author thanks the First Thursday Writers, the Prose Pros,
and the Kirkwood Kibitzers for their advice and support.
She also thanks Mr. George Turner, special consultant on Jamaican culture.

Clarion Books
a Houghton Mifflin Company imprint
215 Park Avenue South, New York, NY 10003
Text copyright © 1997 by Regina Hanson
Illustrations copyright © 1997 by Linda Saport

The illustrations for this book were executed in pastel on paper.
The text is set in 16/20-point Columbus.

Printed in the U.S.A.

Library of Congress Cataloging-in-Publication Data

Hanson, Regina.
The face at the window / by Regina Hanson ; illustrated by Linda Saport.
p.   cm.
Summary: When Dora goes to take a mango from Miss Nella's tree,
she is frightened by the woman's strange behavior.
ISBN 0-395-78625-8
[1. Mental illness—Fiction.   2. Jamaica—Fiction.]   I. Saport, Linda, ill.   II. Title.
PZ7.H1989Fac 1997
[Fic]—dc20   96-3373
CIP
AC

WOZ 10 9 8 7 6 5 4 3 2 1

To all the Alliances for the Mentally Ill, Dr. E. Fuller Torrey,
and to Boulder's Chinook Clubhouse
where warm winds bring welcome change.
—R.H.

For my parents.
—L.S.

Dora whispered, "Shhh!"

She and her friends Lureen and Trevor were hiding behind a big mango tree. The three of them peeked out at a nearby cottage.

Outside the cottage, a woman crouched beside croton bushes. The woman broke off a croton branch and poked the air with it, shouting, "You think you can break into me house? I goin' to fix your business!" She crashed through the bushes, chasing someone only she could see.

Dora's palms tingled with fear as the woman exclaimed, "I have you now, you three-legged beast! Stand still!"

"We better leave quick," Dora whispered.

"Don't move," Trevor whispered back. "Miss Nella soon go inside. Just wait."

Miss Nella danced around her cottage, stumbling on the sloping ground. She struck the porch with the croton branch. Then she went into the cottage.

As Dora inched away from the tree, Lureen grasped her arm and whispered, "We can't leave without mangoes, Dora. De juiciest and sweetest mangoes anywhere!" She dropped several stones into Dora's hand.

Dora looked up into the tree. With the summer mango season over, only a few late fruit remained on the higher, outer branches.

"Mmm. I can taste a mango already," whispered Trevor. Moving away from the tree, he blew on the stones in his hand. Then he brought his arm back and threw. His stone struck leaves. He threw another.

Boof! A mango fell with a thud, startling Dora. Trevor scooped it up as it rolled. He stuffed it into the pocket of his pants.

They hid behind the tree again, listening for Miss Nella. Only the growling of distant thunder broke the silence.

Lureen threw several times and got her mango. She said, "Your turn now, Dora."

Dora looked at the cottage, listening.

"Hurry up, Dora," said Trevor. He eyed gray clouds that blanketed the morning sun. "It goin' to rain."

Dora hesitated.

Lureen said, "You just starting school, Dora, so maybe you too little to be our friend. Or maybe you too scared."

"But is Miss Nella's tree," Dora whispered. "Is Miss Nella's mangoes."

Lureen put her hands on her hips. She said, "Dora, you are de most scaredy-cat girl in de whole of Jamaica. Trevor and I pick mangoes here last year and de year before, and Miss Nella didn't even know."

Trevor said, "If you won't even try to pick a mango, we'll never let you walk to school with us again. Then you will have to walk past Miss Nella's house every day all by your scaredy-cat self!"

Dora crept out from behind the tree, craned her neck so that she could spot a mango, and hurled a stone.

The stone flew high above the tree and disappeared. She threw another. It bounced off a limb and smacked the door of Miss Nella's cottage.

Lureen and Trevor darted away. As Dora ran after them, she heard a creak. She looked back and saw the wooden window of the cottage swinging open. At the window appeared Miss Nella's face.

"I see Miss Nella! And she see me!" gasped Dora as she caught up with Lureen and Trevor.

"I hope you didn't look upon her face," said Trevor.

"I did," said Dora.

Lureen said, "Why you look? Any time Miss Nella show her face at her window, something terrible goin' to happen."

"Yes," said Trevor. "My mama say if you see Miss Nella's face in de window, you in big trouble."

Dora's mouth went dry.

"Miss Nella is one powerful woman," said Lureen. "One *baad* woman. That is what my papa say."

"Yes," said Trevor. "My mama say Miss Nella is a guzu woman who can change children into chickens—chickens with two heads."

Dora's stomach did a somersault. She said, "My pappy say Miss Nella have a sickness."

"So why you afraid of her?" said Lureen.

Dora didn't answer. She wasn't sure what to think. If Pappy was right, and Miss Nella was only sick, why would anybody say unkind things about her? And Miss Nella had such strange and scary ways!

On the rest of the walk to school, Dora couldn't forget Miss Nella's face. In class she saw it in the face of the big round clock on the teacher's desk. And her friend's words still rang in her ears. *Miss Nella is one powerful woman.*

Outside at recess, Lureen and a girl from her class twirled two jump-ropes. Lureen kept the rhythm by calling out,

"Mosquito one,

Mosquito two,

Mosquito jump into hot callaloo!"

Dora joined the line waiting to jump.

As Dora sprang, Lureen yelled,

"Mosquito three,

Mosquito four,

Dora hit Miss Nella's door!"

Everyone on the playground turned to look. Dora's face burned. She forgot to jump, and both ropes got tangled around her legs.

Lureen laughed loudly and sang to Dora,

"Mosquito five,

Mosquito six,

Nella's horse will give you kicks!"

"What you mean?" said Dora. "Miss Nella have no horse."

"Yes," said Trevor. "Miss Nella tell my mama she see a three-legged horse. My mama say Miss Nella go ridin' on de horse every night."

Dora shuddered as she remembered Miss Nella shouting about a three-legged beast.

Pointing at Dora, Lureen said, "De three-legged horse is goin' to get you, Dora! It have two legs behind and one in front. This is how it will sound when it chasing you: Te-cum-tum! Te-cum-tum! Te-cum-tum!"

Dora backed away, trembling.

Lureen said, "I can just see de horse's eyes flashing fire. And I can hear it making a loud banggarang with all de rusty tin cans tied to de legs and tail!"

The other jump-rope twirler dropped her ends of the two ropes and said, "Stop it, Lureen! Why you like to frighten de younger ones so?"

A girl from Dora's class put her arm around Dora's shoulders. Dora said, "You, Lureen. And you, Trevor. You not me friends. I goin' to walk home alone."

After school Dora hurried along the road. Black clouds wheeled across the sky. The air felt heavy. No birds sang. Near Miss Nella's, Dora began to run. As she sprinted past the cottage, she heard a creak. Without thinking she glanced back. At the open window of the cottage appeared Miss Nella's face.

"*Wai-oh!*" Dora wailed. "I see her again!" Running all the way home, she was sure she heard the three-legged horse chasing her. *Te-cum-tum! Te-cum-tum! Te-cum-tum!*

As Dora sprinkled finely chopped coconut for the chickens in her yard, her hands shook. She checked to make sure none of the chickens had two heads. When raindrops pelted the ground, the chickens scurried into their coop. The donkey and two goats found shelter in the cooking hut behind the house. Dora dashed indoors.

She watched as rain painted the green hills white. Raindrops beating the metal roof of her house sounded like a hundred drums. Water gurgled in the bamboo gutters and splashed into the big storage barrels. Darkness came suddenly, and Mammy lit the kerosene-oil lamps.

Pappy said, "What a heavy rain! Is like a hurricane!"

Now the rain pounded the roof so loudly that Dora covered her ears with her hands. She remembered what Lureen had said. *Any time Miss Nella show her face at her window, something terrible goin' to happen.*

This is only rain, thought Dora. We get rain often enough. Nothing terrible about that. But as the rain grew louder on the roof, Dora's stomach tightened.

Mammy looked up at the rafters and said, "What a banggarang!"

Dora jumped with fright. She cried, "Is de three-legged horse on de roof!" She threw herself into Mammy's arms and burst into tears.

"No such thing as three-legged horse," said Pappy.

"But I can hear it bouncin' up there," said Dora. "Te-cum-tum! Te-cum-tum! Te-cum-tum!"

Mammy hugged Dora. "Listen with me now," said Mammy. "You hear that? Is only rain. And it soon stop."

But the rain did not stop. At bedtime Dora peered out her window. For a moment, she thought she saw a huge horse galloping toward her, its eyes flashing fire. Then, as lightning lit up the yard, the horse vanished. Shivering, Dora crept into bed and pulled the sheet over her head.

Rain drumming on the roof woke her the next morning. She was glad that it was Saturday and she didn't have to walk past Miss Nella's to school. But worry still gnawed at her stomach. She stayed close to Mammy and Pappy.

The longer the rain poured, the more certain Dora became that Lureen had been right when she said, "Something terrible goin' to happen." Something terrible *is* happening, thought Dora. And now I have to tell.

"De rain never goin' to end," she said. "And is all my fault."

"Why you say so?" Pappy asked.

Dora stared at the floor. She said, "Yesterday I try to pick one of Miss Nella's mangoes with a stone, and I hit her door by mistake."

Pappy looked up from the basket he was weaving. Mammy frowned at her sewing.

Dora told them everything. Then she said, "Miss Nella make this terrible rain come because I make her angry. Lureen and Trevor say Miss Nella is a powerful woman, a bad woman."

"No-no, Dora girl," said Pappy. "Miss Nella not bad at all. I don't understand her sickness, but it is inside her head."

Mammy touched Dora's head, saying, "Miss Nella's mind play tricks on her. Sometimes she see and hear things that are not there."

Dora asked, "So how come some people say she bad?"

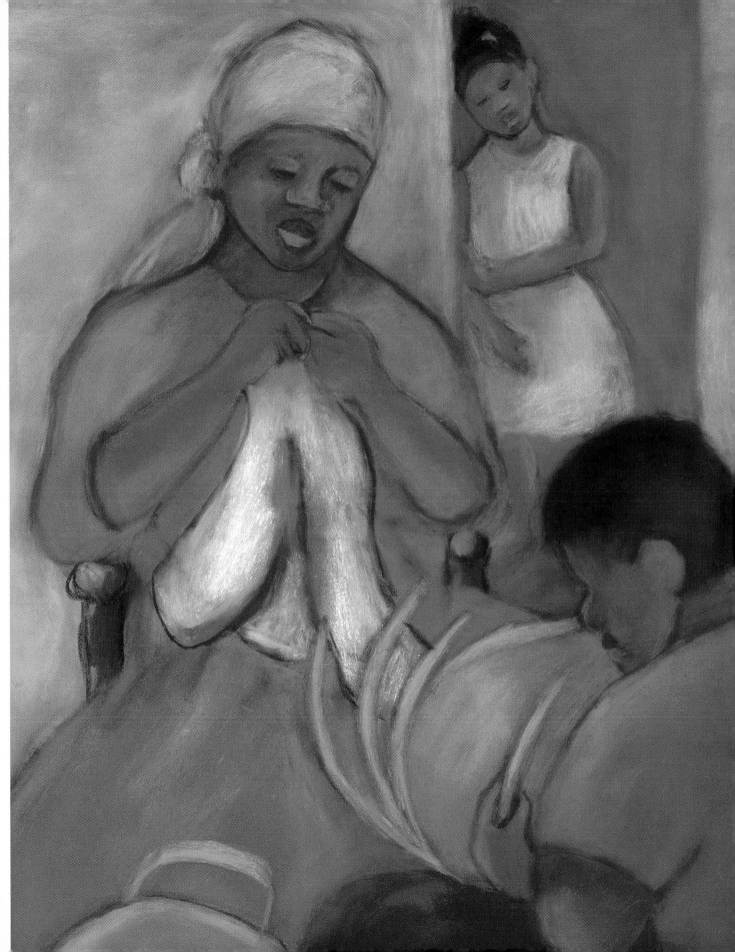

Mammy set aside the dress she was mending and drew Dora onto her lap. "Some people afraid of what they don't understand," said Mammy.

Dora said, "So why de doctor don't make her better?"

"I don't know," said Pappy. "But I know one thing. Miss Nella cannot cause rain. Rain come when it ready."

"You sure?" said Dora.

"Sure-sure," said Pappy.

Taking Dora's hand, Mammy said, "Dora girl, you think you should do anything about hittin' Miss Nella's door with a stone and tryin' to take her mangoes?"

"I should tell Miss Nella I sorry," Dora answered. "But I afraid to go to her!"

Pappy said, "Mammy and I will walk with you when de rain is over."

Then Mammy said, "Maybe we all need something to sweeten up this gloomy day." She went to the cupboard and brought out the jar in which she kept tamarind balls.

Pappy and Mammy each took a tamarind ball, and they gave Dora the last two in the jar.

Dora ate one. Today she tasted the sour tamarind, but not the sugar that she and Mammy had used to sweeten it. Maybe it would taste better later, she thought. She wrapped the last tamarind ball in her kerchief and tucked it into the pocket of her skirt.

The next day Dora awoke to silence. "De rain stop!" she exclaimed, and she went out to her porch. The hills wore caps of fluffy cloud, and silver mists slept in the valleys. Dora smelled smoke from the breakfast fires and her mouth watered. Then she remembered. Today she had to go to Miss Nella's. Dora didn't feel hungry anymore.

On the way to Miss Nella's, Dora walked slowly between Mammy and Pappy. She said, "You promise to stay right beside me when we reach her house?"

"Yes," said Mammy.

Still, Dora's hands felt cold. She stopped walking. "I can't go!" she said. "Lureen and Trevor say something terrible will happen to anybody who look at Miss Nella's face!"

"I look at Miss Nella's face plenty of times," said Pappy. "And nothing terrible happen to me because of it."

"For true?" said Dora.

"True-true," said Pappy. "When I was a boy, me mama had a weak heart. Sometimes, when me papa was out plantin' de ground, Miss Nella come to de house with coconut water for me mama to drink. And while me mama was restin', Miss Nella show me how to make baskets."

When they reached the path to Miss Nella's cottage, Dora gripped Mammy's hand, and Pappy's, too.

Standing on Miss Nella's porch, Dora felt her heart racing. She knocked on the door.

A shaky voice spoke from inside the cottage. "Is who that?"

Dora could hardly breathe. She answered, "Is de girl who . . . who hit your door . . . with a stone."

Feet shuffled toward the door. As it opened, Dora pressed close against Mammy and looked down so that she wouldn't see Miss Nella's face. Her heartbeat pounded in her ears, louder, louder, like the drumming of heavy rain on the roof of her house, like the sound of the three-legged horse. *Te-cum-tum! Te-cum-tum! Te-cum-tum!*

Miss Nella said, "Ah! Is me friend! How de basket-makin' goin' on?"

Still looking down, Dora realized that Miss Nella was talking to Pappy.

"De baskets goin' well, thanks," said Pappy. "Me daughter come to see you. Is Dora."

"So her name is Dora," said Miss Nella. "Dora is de girl whose stones have wings!"

Dora squeezed her eyelids shut and said, "I come to say . . . to say sorry. For de stones. And de mangoes." She held her breath.

When Miss Nella didn't answer, Dora couldn't help opening one eye, just the tiniest bit, for one instant, to steal a glance at her.

Miss Nella had cocked her head to one side. She exclaimed, "Listen! Can you hear de noise?" She rushed into the yard and knelt to put her ear to the ground. "De crabs are marchin' over de land," she muttered. "I hear all de crabs' legs—thousands of legs—tappin' de earth. Can you hear de crabs talkin'?"

Mammy and Pappy went out to Miss Nella. "Is all right, Miss Nella," Pappy said, stroking her shoulder. "Everything all right."

Dora tiptoed into the yard. Kneeling behind Pappy and Mammy, she put her ear to the ground. She heard nothing.

Miss Nella covered her ears with her hands and cried, "De crabs sayin' they comin' to get us!"

When Dora heard the fear in Miss Nella's voice, her breath caught. She whispered to Mammy, "Miss Nella can hear de crabs, but they not really there. Is like when I think I hear de three-legged horse on our roof!"

Mammy whispered, "Yes," and squeezed Dora's hand.

Except, thought Dora, the sound of the horse did stop after I talk to Mammy and Pappy about it. But maybe Miss Nella can't stop the noise of the crabs. And she live alone without anybody to tell her is O.K.

Miss Nella rocked on her knees, saying, "De crabs comin'."

Still not looking at Miss Nella's face, Dora said from behind Pappy, "You safe, Miss Nella. Safe."

"You sure?" said Miss Nella.

"Sure-sure," said Dora.

Miss Nella paced the yard, muttering. Then she went into her cottage.

"Maybe is time we go, Miss Nella," Pappy called.

After several moments, Miss Nella called, "Hold on." She came out again, cradling a mango in both hands. She held it out to Dora, saying, "For de girl whose stones have wings!"

Dora climbed onto the porch and took the mango. The golden mango smell tickled her nose. She said, "Thank you, Miss Nella," and wished she had something to give Miss Nella in return.

Then she remembered the tamarind ball in her pocket. She handed the mango to Mammy, pulled out the kerchief, and offered the tamarind ball to Miss Nella. And, without thinking about it, Dora looked up into Miss Nella's face.

Miss Nella had kind eyes. Her face lit up when she popped the tamarind ball into her mouth. She said, "Mm-hm. Is good."

As Dora, Mammy, and Pappy walked toward the road, Dora
said, "Let's make more tamarind balls. Just for Miss Nella."
"She will like that," said Pappy.
When they reached the road, Dora glanced back.
At the window of the cottage appeared Miss Nella's face.
Dora turned toward Miss Nella and waved good-bye.